CREEPY RIDDLES

Katy Hall and Lisa Eisenberg

pictures by S. D. Schindler

PUFFIN BOOKS

PUFFIN BOOKS
Published by the Penguin Group
Penguin Putnam Books for Young Readers, 345 Hudson Street, New York, New York 10014, U.S.A.
Penguin Books Ltd, 27 Wrights Lane, London W8 5TZ, England
Penguin Books Australia Ltd, Ringwood, Victoria, Australia
Penguin Books Canada Ltd, 10 Alcorn Avenue, Toronto, Ontario, Canada M4V 3B2
Penguin Books (N.Z.) Ltd, 182-190 Wairau Road, Auckland 10, New Zealand

Penguin Books Ltd, Registered Offices: Harmondsworth, Middlesex, England

First published in the United States of America by Dial Books for Young Readers,
a member of Penguin Putnam Inc., 1998
Published by Puffin Books, a division of Penguin Putnam Books for Young Readers, 2000

1 3 5 7 9 10 8 6 4 2

THE LIBRARY OF CONGRESS HAS CATALOGED THE DIAL EDITION AS FOLLOWS:
Hall, Katy.
Creepy riddles/by Katy Hall and Lisa Eisenberg;
pictures by S. D. Schindler.
p. cm.
ISBN 0-8037-1684-2 (tr.)—ISBN 0-8037-1685-0 (lib.)
1. Riddles. 2. Supernatural—Juvenile humor.
[1. Riddles. 2. Supernatural—Wit and humor.] I. Eisenberg, Lisa. II. Schindler, S. D., ill. III. Title.
PN6371.5.H375 1998 818'.5402—DC20 94-37524 CIP AC r94

Puffin Easy-to-Read ISBN 0-14-130988-1
Puffin® and Easy-to-Read® are registered trademarks of Penguin Putnam Inc.

Printed in Hong Kong

The full-color artwork was prepared using pen-and-ink and watercolor washes.

Reading Level 2.1

To Lisa Eisenberg
K.H.
To Katy Hall
L.E.

To Julia—still a riddle, but not a creepy one!
S.D.S.

What do werewolves
say when they meet?

"Howl do you do?"

What do you call a room full of ghosts?

A bunch of boo-boos!

How do skeletons
send their mail?

By Bony Express.

What do witches like to eat
for dessert?

Ice scream!

Why does Dracula buy the newspaper every night?

So he can read his horror-scope.

Why do witches
wear green eye shadow?

They like the way
it matches their teeth.

What moves through the air, casts spells, and has no name?

An unidentified flying sorcerer.

How did
the monster football team
win the game?

They kicked a field ghoul!

What would you get
if you crossed a skeleton
and a jar of peanut butter?

Bones that stick to the
roof of your mouth!

What kind of stories
do little ghosts tell
around the campfire?

People stories.

How did the werewolf
send his valentines?

By hairmail!

Which witches like to play croquet?

Wicket witches!

How does a witch
with a broken broom
get to the second floor?

She takes the scarecase.

Why did the little fiends join the protest march?

They thought it was a *demon*stration.

Why didn't the little skeleton
want to go to the party?

Because he had no
body to dance with!

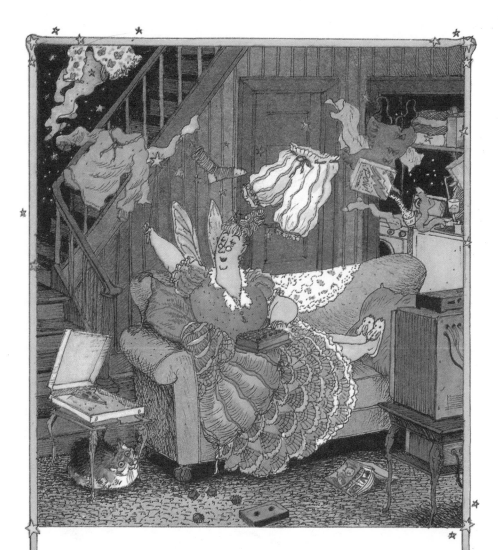

What magic words
does a scary godmother
use to do her laundry?

"Wishy-washy!"

What do ghosts love to eat
for dinner?

Ghoulash.

Why is Frankenstein
so helpful?

He's always willing
to give you a hand!

Why did Granny Monster
knit her grandson three socks?

Because she heard
he'd grown another foot.

Where do demons go at night?

Out with their ghoulfriends!

What do sea monsters
like to eat?

Fish-and-ships!

What did the little ghost order at the restaurant?

Spookghetti!

What do zombies like to drink?

*Croak*a-Cola!

Why are witch twins
so confusing?

You can never tell
which witch is which!

Why did the Frankenstein monster get a tummy ache?

He kept *bolting* his food!

What color is a chilly ghost?

Boo!

What trees do zombies
like best?

Ceme-trees!

What do ghouls like to do at the amusement park?

Ride the roller ghoster!

What do vampires eat
at baseball games?

Fangfurters!

Why is the mad scientist
never lonely?

He's good at *making*
new friends!

Why did everyone call
the vampire crazy?

They heard he'd gone batty!

What do ghosts put on their mashed potatoes?

Grave-y!

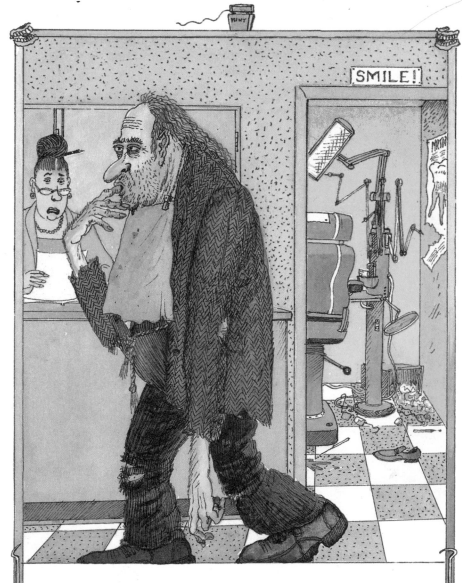

What did the zombie eat
after he had a tooth taken out?

The dentist!

What fairy tale is scary enough
to tell little witches?

Ghouldilocks and the Three Scares.

Why did Frankenstein fall in love with the witch?

She *swept* him off his feet!

Why did the little witch get a prize in school?

She was the best *spell*er in her class.

What game do little zombies
play at birthday parties?

Swallow the leader!

What do you get if you cross a giant with a vampire?

A *big* pain in the neck!

What did the little vampire
say to the judges when he won
the Batboy Contest?

"Fangs a lot!"

What did the ghost bride
throw to her bridesmaids?

Her *boo*quet!